Here Comes Santa Claus

A♭ A♮dim E♭ C7 Fm B♭7
Bells are ring - ing, chil - dren sing - sing, All is mer - ry and
Hear those sleigh - bells jin - gle jan - gle, What a beau - ti - ful
Sant - a knows that we're God's chil - dren— That makes ev - 'ry - thing—
Peace on earth will come to all If we just fol - low the
mf
E♭ E♭7 A♭ A♮dim E♭ C7
bright. Hang your stock - ings and say your pray'rs, 'Cause
sight. Jump in bed, cov - er up your head, 'Cause
right. Fill your hearts with a Christ - mas cheer, 'Cause
light. Let's give thanks to the Lord a - bove, 'Cause
1, 2, 3
Fm B♭7 E♭ B♭7
1.
2. Sant - a Claus comes to - night.
3.
4
Fm B♭7 E♭
4. Sant - a Claus comes to - night.
Fine

Here Comes Santa Claus

For information address HarperCollins Children's Books, a division of HarperCollins Publishers, 1350 Avenue of the Americas, New York, NY 10019.
www.harpercollinschildrens.com

Library of Congress Cataloging-in-Publication Data
Autry, Gene, 1907–
Here comes Santa Claus / words and music by Gene Autry and Oakley Haldeman ; illustrated by Bruce Whatley.
p. cm.
Summary: Santa Claus is riding down Santa Claus Lane tonight with toys for all girls and boys.
ISBN 978-0-06-028268-4 (trade bdg.) — ISBN 978-0-06-028269-1 (lib. bdg.)
ISBN 978-0-06-443545-1 (pbk.)
1. Christmas music—Texts. 2. Children's songs—Texts. [1. Santa Claus—Songs and music. 2. Christmas music. 3. Songs.] I. Haldeman, Oakley, 1911–
II. Whatley, Bruce, ill. III. Title.
PZ8.3.A9375 He 2002
782.42'1723'0268—dc21 2001039373
[E] CIP
AC

Typography by Al Cetta ❖ First Edition

Here Comes Santa Claus

WORDS AND MUSIC

BY GENE AUTRY

AND OAKLEY HALDEMAN

ILLUSTRATED BY

BRUCE WHATLEY

Here comes Santa Claus! Here comes Santa Claus!
Right down Santa Claus Lane!
Vixen and Blitzen and all his reindeer
Are pulling on the rein.

Silent Night

Bells are ringing, children singing,
All is merry and bright.

Santa

Hang your stockings and say your prayers,
'Cause Santa Claus comes tonight.

Here comes Santa Claus! Here comes Santa Claus!
Right down Santa Claus Lane!
He's got a bag that is filled with toys
For the boys and girls again.

Hear those sleigh bells jingle jangle,
What a beautiful sight.

Jump in bed, cover up your head,
'Cause Santa Claus comes tonight.

Here comes Santa Claus! Here comes Santa Claus!
Right down Santa Claus Lane!
He doesn't care if you're rich or poor
For he loves you just the same.

Santa knows that we're God's children—
That makes everything right.

Dear Santa,
I know I already
asked for a real
genuine Cowboy hat
but what I really
want for Christmas
is a puppy.
Your friend,
Matthew

Fill your hearts with a Christmas cheer,
'Cause Santa Claus comes tonight.

Here comes Santa Claus! Here comes Santa Claus!
Right down Santa Claus Lane!
He'll come around when the chimes ring out—
Then it's Christmas morn again.

Peace on Earth will come to all
If we just follow the light.

Dear Matthew
This is Tinsel. She is a
very special puppy.
Give her loving care.
Merry Christmas
Santa

Let's give thanks to the Lord above,
'Cause Santa Claus comes tonight!

Here Comes Santa Claus

A♭ A♮dim E♭ C7 Fm B♭7
Bells are ring - ing, chil - dren sing - sing, All is mer - ry and
Hear those sleigh - bells jin - gle jan - gle, What a beau - ti - ful
Sant - a knows that we're God's chil - dren— That makes ev - 'ry - thing—
Peace on earth will come to all If we just fol - low the
mf
E♭ E♭7 A♭ A♮dim E♭ C7
bright. Hang your stock - ings and say your pray'rs, 'Cause
sight. Jump in bed, cov - er up your head, 'Cause
right. Fill your hearts with a Christ - mas cheer, 'Cause
light. Let's give thanks to the Lord a - bove, 'Cause
1, 2, 3
Fm B♭7 E♭ B♭7
1. 2. 3. Sant - a Claus comes to - night.
4
Fm B♭7 E♭
4. Sant - a Claus comes to - night.
Fine